I0782226

In my Father's Garden

LISA C. MURPHY

Illustrations by Liza Brown

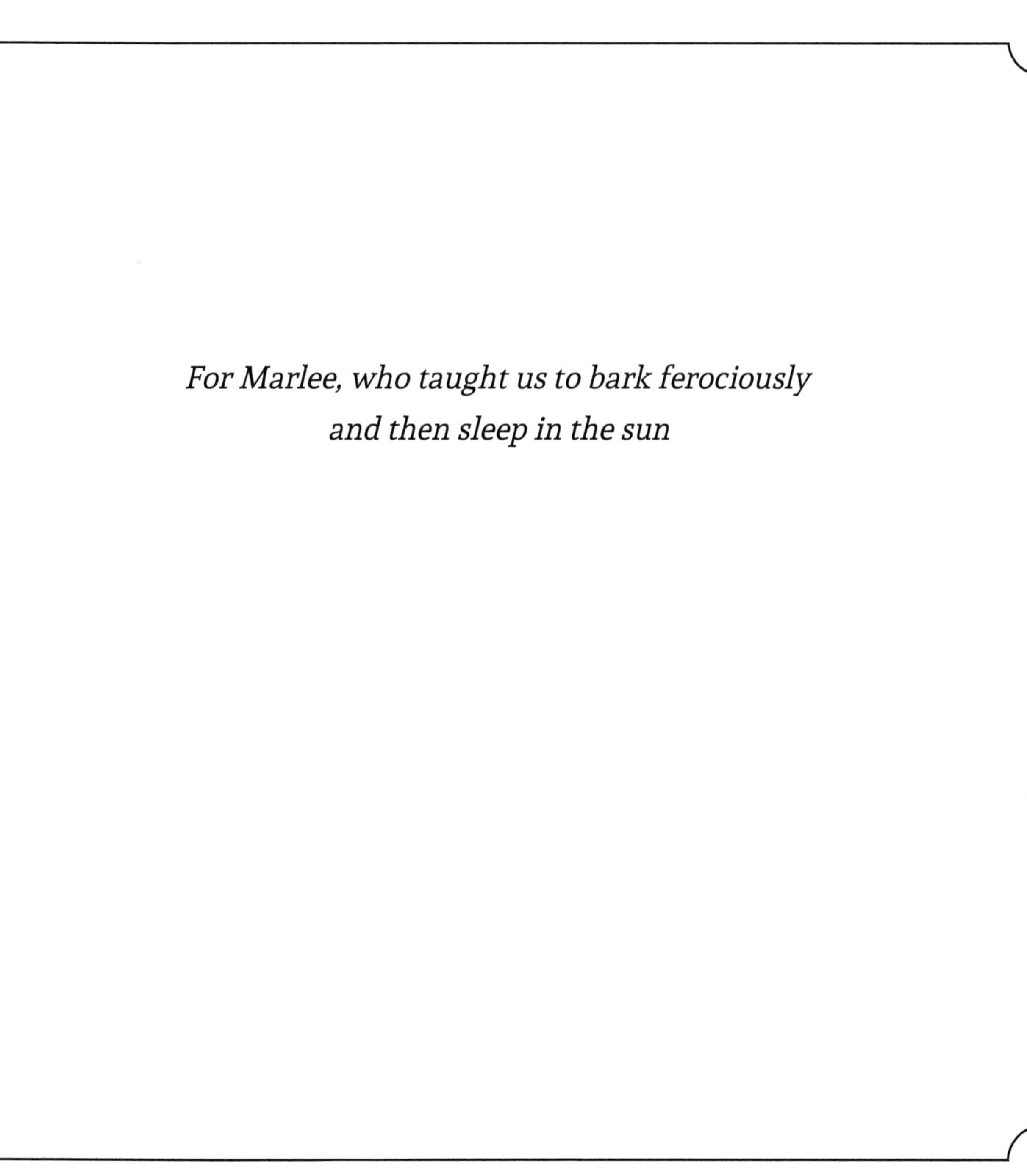

*For Marlee, who taught us to bark ferociously
and then sleep in the sun*

The Crow

In my father's garden there lived a big black crow. He peered over the rain gutters, picked the sprouts from our vegetable patch, and left dead bugs in our birdbath. He was a real pain. Every time our dog, Marlee, went into the garden the bird would screech and caw. Marlee didn't like the crow a bit, barking and howling whenever she caught sight of him. If she wasn't on a leash she'd go after him, dashing in circles as if she were demented. When the two of them got going they made a terrible racket, chasing each other around and around the garden—a wild chaos that often woke my father from his nap.

One day Marlee wasn't on her leash. She was an older dog who enjoyed lying around in the sun. She was sleepy, carelessly stretched out, taking her usual pleasure in watching the murmuring bees.

The crow peeked over the gutter and spied her. The lounging dog was too sweet of a temptation, and like a flash he attacked.

Marlee leapt to her feet and took up the chase, yipping and barking. She was nearly upon him when she suddenly howled to a stop. The crow flew off and perched himself on a telephone wire. He sat there and studied the dog, who clearly could no longer walk. What a clever trick, making a dog run until she'd strained a leg! The crow chirred to himself as if absolutely delighted.

For six weeks poor Marlee was disabled. Thanks to the crow, she lay about the house or limped slowly here and there, reluctant to go outside. The crow peered through our living room window, cocking his head to one side. Why wasn't the dog in the garden? He had the garden all to himself now. Fantastic! He seemed very pleased with how well things had worked out.

Unfortunately, bad luck waited for the crow as well.

In Washington State we have hundreds of bald eagles. They steal eggs from the crows' nests, kill the nestlings, and hunt mercilessly for any sick birds. As you might expect, crows aren't very fond of bald eagles. Whenever

they see one they gather with neighboring crows and mob the predator with all their combined strength. Several times a week they risk their lives to protect their flock. Our crow was fearless in his pursuit of bald eagles.

One day, shortly after Marlee had finally healed, a large bald eagle flew over the house. Our crow raced into the sky with all the other crows, taking the eagle on. But this was a windy day and a gust blew our crow underneath the eagle. The eagle's claws closed over him. The crow struggled, cawing desperately, dragging the eagle from side to side until he finally managed to free himself. Tumbling head over heels, he fell into our garden.

Marlee—who must have seen the crow fall—barked furiously to get out. She sniffed around the garden until she found him lying under the rose bushes. With frantic yips she alerted me, and I hurried to pick him up. The crow lay quietly in my hands, ragged and mangled, watching me with no trace of fear.

We're friends, his eyes seemed to say. *Help me!*

What else could we do?

Marlee and I brought the crow to the wild animal shelter. The dog waited in the car, running back and forth from window to window as I spoke to the veterinarian. Unfortunately, both of our crow's legs were broken, so I had no choice but to leave him there. I paid the shelter to care for him, but it didn't seem possible that a bird with two broken legs could survive.

Meanwhile, all the crows in our neighborhood were in a tizzy. Where was our crow? Why didn't he rush into the sky whenever an eagle flew over? They gathered on the telephone wires around our house. They peered over the rain gutters and into our windows. Whenever Marlee and my father took a walk, a cawing host of birds followed them. They were irate, that was loud and clear, convinced we were responsible for our crow's disappearance. After three weeks of this harassment we received a letter from the shelter; they were very sorry, but our crow had died.

We were devastated: our brave, saucy crow would never hop in our garden again. My father couldn't even bury him under the roses.

We went into mourning.

Eventually, the other crows forgot their fury and our garden was quiet. Marlee was bored and laid around the house with nothing to occupy her, no one to chase. It was going to be a long summer.

Then one day, about a month later, a young crow came into the garden. He landed on the roof and peered over the rain gutter. He yanked out the vegetable sprouts, then hopped into the birdbath. Hey, he decided, our garden wasn't too bad! Soon we'd have dead bugs in the birdbath again and hear the usual fearful din. Seeing the crow, Marlee leapt to her feet and ran, barking and tail wagging, out into the garden. But this wasn't a warning; it was a friendly welcome.

ಱಱಱ

The Worm Bin

In my father's garden we had many roses. The yellow roses climbed over the fence and fell in waves into our neighbor's garden. The white roses intertwined with the pink roses. The red ones sprang up between our other flowers. We gave the blooms away to friends and set large bouquets on our kitchen table. The petals fell everywhere, giving the house a wonderful scent. The garden was lovely, but it hadn't always been that way.

Gardeners know: without decent compost, roses grow slowly, bloom abysmally, and catch black spot. After a warm night's rain white mildew appears on the leaves, making the bushes unattractive. To cure these woes I decided to get a worm composter.

A worm composter is just a box to hold rotting vegetables. At first glance

it isn't complicated. But wooden worm bins decompose over time. Plastic bins are too cold in the winter for the poor worms and have to be dragged inside the house. There they leave a stinking brown mess of slime everywhere.

Given the complications, I decided to seek professional advice. Fortunately I had a friend who was a horticulturist, and she gave me the name of a woman who specialized in worm composters. This specialist lived not very far from my house.

As it turned out, not quite far enough.

At first all went well. I called her and we set up a time to meet. She asked me to come to her house so she could show me her worm bins.

She lived in a hovel with a mossy old roof and cracking stucco on the walls. Her house might not have been much, but her garden was breathtaking. Even in early spring, winter still breathing down our necks, her plants bloomed and thrived. Golden narcissus thrust up from the ground, decorating the entire landscape. The apple trees were so laden with blooms that their branches sagged. Tulips formed a barrier around the house as thick as a wall. There was

no doubt of her skill as a gardener. I was thrilled; maybe my father's garden could be as magnificent.

She explained to me that her favorite worm composter cost forty dollars. She could sell me one. Worms cost twenty-five dollars a pound. According to her, I needed a pound.

Her composters stood outside under the trees near her garden shed. There, she lifted the first tray of one of her bins and began to give a lecture. Every aspect of the bin required an explanation: the right type of rotting vegetables; the perfect soil; the dangerous insects that grubbed in the dirt; the moisture that could drown the worms; the dreadful heat of summer, and the menacing freezes that came with fall. For almost an hour I stood in the brisk breeze and suffered through her monologue on the many trials and tribulations that came with owning a worm bin.

It began to rain and water leaked into my shoes. My fingers were frozen. Still, she had more to say. Finally, I couldn't stand anymore and interrupted her. Did she have any brochures that I could read? Of course she did! In fact, for only fifteen dollars, she'd sell me an entire book. To save myself from dying of the

cold, I bought the book. Eighty dollars and ten frozen fingers later, I finally took my worm box, book, and pound of worms and went home. Thank heavens I'd escaped! Done is done, I figured. Now I could enjoy my composter in peace. Boy was I mistaken.

The next day I put my composter together, filling it with shredded newspaper and dirt. I tossed in old vegetable and fruit scraps—without any citrus peelings, as the worm lady had instructed. I mixed everything together and dumped in the worms. Excellent: a beautiful worm bin! I was very pleased. I set it in a safe place near the garden wall. All was ready. In a few months we'd have fabulous compost.

That evening I received an email. My worm lady wanted to know if my bin was doing well.

"Yes," I replied. "It's wonderful."

She didn't write any response.

Then, a week later, I came home and saw a shadow in my father's garden. It was night and very dark. Cautiously I approached, creeping up slowly and

carefully. A person was leaning over the worm composter.

 "Who's there?" I asked.

She turned around. It was the worm lady! She clicked on a flashlight, shining it into the box.

"It's too wet in there," she said. "Did you put water in it?"

"N-n-no!" I stammered. "No water. The vegetable scraps were wet."

"Too wet," she pronounced. "The worms need more shredded paper."

She nodded. Then she went off down our driveway, found her car, and drove away.

I stood there, astounded. She'd dared to come into my father's garden and continue her sermon! I'd never seen such audacity. Angry and somewhat bemused, I went into the house. Finding a flashlight, I returned to the garden. She was right; there was too much moisture in the box. Worms lay on the surface in an effort to escape being drowned. I mixed in more shredded paper then went off to bed. Lying there, I wondered about the worm lady. What might she do next?

For a month I awaited her return, but she didn't come back. I breathed a sigh of relief.

Perhaps she'd exhausted her ability to harangue me—I could only hope. Then, early one morning, I had scraps for the composter and came out into the garden. The worm bin was gone. Vanished. I searched the entire garden, top to bottom; it had disappeared into thin air. For heaven's sake, who would steal a worm bin? The garden tools were still there. The watering hoses were there. Nothing else seemed to be missing. What the heck?

Then I saw a dark object deep in the bushes, well hidden behind the tangled branches. I approached and peered through the leaves. It was the worm bin with a note stuck on top.

Dear Ms. Murphy,

Summer is coming and the wall will be too hot for the worm composter. I took it upon myself to move it, so as not to roast the worms in the heat.

Fondly,

Z.H.

Well, I thought, I'll be darned. Unbelievable. Perhaps she was right—it was warm up against the wall—but this bordered on crazy. What could I do? Again, I lay awake that night, worrying about the worm lady. She made me nervous. I had to get rid of her somehow, but how?

For the whole summer, the worm bin stayed in the bushes. In order to fill it, I had to crawl through the branches, twigs scratching my skin. It was a real pain, not my favorite activity, but the worms thrived. I knew that the worm lady would come back—it was too much to ask for her to go away—but I didn't see any sign of her.

Then finally in the fall, I returned from work one evening to find a package by the door. It was a large, strangely shaped bundle about as big as I was. I dragged it into the house and went to find a knife to cut it open. Inside was a roll of bubble wrap. Bubble wrap? Why bubble wrap? I looked for a return address, but there wasn't one. I unrolled the wrap and looked for note. No note. What was I supposed to do with this? It was so bizarre, it could only be from the worm lady. I stuck it in the front hall closet and waited. Two days later, I received a letter:

Dear Ms. Murphy,

Winter is coming, and your worms need protection from the cold. Please encase the worm bin in bubble wrap. You owe me twenty dollars for the insulation and postage.

Fondly,

Z.H.

That was the last straw. I couldn't tolerate this any longer. I repacked the bubble wrap, wrote her address with "return to sender" on the label, and took the package to the post office. Then I hid the worm bin in the garage, locked the door, and wrote her back:

Dear Z.H.,

I've given up my worm bin. It was too much work. I no longer need your assistance.

Fondly,

L.M.

I mailed the letter off. Over the next few weeks there were hints that the worm lady had been by, poking around. Where the worm bin had stood, twigs were broken from the bushes. There were small footprints here and there in the mud, as if a garden gnome had visited. But I never saw her.

For the whole winter the worm bin stayed, safe and sound, in the garage. Come spring, I decided not to drag it back outside again. True, it dripped stinky brown water everywhere. But despite the mess, I would leave it where the rain couldn't make it too moist and the sun couldn't roast it. Most importantly, the worm lady couldn't find it.

For two years I hid the worm bin. The worms did well. Then, one spring day, I decided to organize the garage. I dragged the bin back out into the garden. The trees had grown up over the years, and the wall was no longer in the sun. Thick branches now protected the bin from the rain. The wall had become a perfect home for the worms, so I set the composter there. Over time, my father's roses had profited from the compost with gorgeous blooms, free of disease. What a wonderful garden my father had! I was proud and gave full credit to the worm bin.

Three days later the worm lady was at the door. Why was I surprised? I should have expected her. Heedless of the danger, I invited her into the house.

"Have a seat," I said. "Would you like some tea?"

"Yes, please."

There was an awkward silence while the water boiled.

I set her cup on the table.

"Ms. H., I have a confession to make. I never gave up my worm bin. It was in the garage."

"I figured as much."

"I hid it from you because you are so meddlesome."

She gave me a sad smile. "You aren't the first to say so."

"Listen to me, my worms have done very well for years. Do you think could bring yourself to quit spying on me?"

She stared at her hands for a moment then met my gaze. "I agree, you've taken good care of your worms. I won't bother you anymore." Then she finished her tea, stood up, and went to the door.

"Goodbye, Ms. H.," I said.

"Goodbye."

She turned to go down the front steps, then she turned back and gave me a mischievous smile. "Would you like a Mason bee house? I have Mason bees that don't have any stingers. I could show you how to take care of them."

You can imagine what I thought... *Never in a zillion years!*

"Thanks, Ms. H.," I said. "But really, no thanks."

ෲෲෲ

A Plague of Hummingbirds

In my father's garden there are many flowers that hummingbirds love: fuchsia, beebalm, penstemon, crocosmia, and sage. Every July, when everything is blooming, the garden buzzes with these beautiful little birds.

I used to believe that hummingbirds were delicate, tiny wonders—frail and vulnerable. Then, one February, a female Anna's hummingbird made a nest low in the evergreen tree that stood in my father's garden. Thanks to that nest, I've significantly revised my opinion.

A hummingbird's mating dance is dramatic and stormy. The male shoots up more than one hundred feet into the sky. Then he swoops down in an arc, chittering, pulling up at the last moment before hitting the ground.

Apparently females find this dance attractive, for they flock to the wildest and loudest displays. We had this sort of aggressive male in our garden, and because of him, a female arrived to build a nest.

When I saw the female hummingbird I was delighted. In an effort to help, I set out sugar water and a wire basket with dryer lint that she could use for her nest. Then I watched from the window as she sipped from the feeder and carried the lint around, flitting from branch to branch. Soon we would have a whole family of hummingbirds buzzing around the garden. It was thrilling.

Our resident crow also noticed the nest. He peered over the rain gutter, laying his head to one side as he looked the situation over. Soon he began to creep nearer, chirring softly, lurking in the branches overhead. At first I figured he was curious. Then it occurred to me that he might be hungry: baby hummingbirds would make a good snack.

I might have been worried about the crow, but the mother hummingbird seemed unconcerned. She flitted around him as though he were a harmless

blob. He inched closer to the nesting site, but she ignored him. Throughout all of this, the male hummingbird appeared to have forgotten his partner. He went on living his life without any apparent thought for the nest at all. It seemed to me that the babies would be eaten as soon as they were born.

A male Anna's hummingbird is a beautiful creature with a blood-red throat and head. His back is a shimmering green and his chest is soft white. The female has none of these striking colors. She is a drab and forgettable gray-green and can hide well in her natural environment. Such a tiny little bird could be almost invisible, especially sitting still on a branch. Often, it seemed to me, the crow was unaware that the female was there; the female could sneak up behind him without him knowing. And so the nest was built: the crow circling the nest, and the hummingbird circling the crow.

No sooner was the nest finished, than the mother laid two little eggs. The eggs were white and as small as a fingertip, two tiny pearls. Now she never left her brood. Because the little cup of twigs, moss, and lint was only one and a half inches wide, she could cover the entire thing with her body.

She hunched there, her pointed bill aimed toward the crow, her beady eyes watching. The crow, who had had no trouble with the hummingbird to date, apparently saw no danger in her posture. He continued his dance of coming up to the nest and then flitting away, daring to approach ever closer.

Somehow the mother bird survived the gestation of her eggs without disaster. The babies hatched and began to peep. I could hear their soft little voices as I gardened. Now the crow was always at their doorstep. As he could be in the nest in a flash, it was never safe to leave it alone. How could the mother feed herself and her babies? I refilled the sugar water and hoped.

Then, a few days after the babies were born, I was weeding the perennial beds and heard a terrible racket. I looked up in the evergreen and there was the crow. He was poking at the moss of the nest with his bill, trying to get a hold on the babies. The nestlings were screaming bloody murder, defending themselves wildly against the attack. The mother was nowhere to be seen. I sprang up,

garden hoe in hand, and ran for the tree. I was about to hit the crow when a whirring, buzzing storm of wings attacked him. The crow gave a surprised squawk, unable to get a bead on what was after him. In an effort to escape, he hopped to another branch. Again and again he was pecked, feathers blinding him. He fought back with claws and beak, but the mother hummingbird was too nimble. Finally, he took to the sky, the hummingbird fast on his tail. Their shrieking could be heard for a long time before it faded into the distance.

Great, I thought. That solves that problem.

My heavens, was I ever wrong.

A few minutes later the mother was back, and she was furious. Dive-bombing my head, whistling by my ears, she attacked me with everything she had. She drove me across the lawn, pursuing me until I hid myself in the house. She didn't care that I had defended her nest: no one dared trespass in her garden.

For the next few weeks, our garden was off limits. Every time one of us went outside, she would attack. Not my father nor my husband, our friends, or even our dog Marlee could come and go safely. We were the enemy.

The nestlings grew up, learned to fly, and figured out how to use the sugar-water feeder. Still, we weren't welcome. Now they were mature enough to buzz about, and three hummingbirds pursued us whenever we went outside. I had to refill the sugar water at night. From the sanctuary of our living room, we stood in the window and watched the weeds grow tall.

Finally, the grownup nestlings flew away. The mother hummingbird, alone now, forgot her fury and returned to her normal self. We breathed a collective sigh of relief, and my father and I picked up our garden hoes. A few days later, the poor crow slunk cautiously back into the yard, giving the hummingbird a wide berth.

So, the next year, did I lure in hummingbirds with sugar water and dryer lint? Mmm. . . no. They may look beautiful and delightful, but they are really little terrors with wings.

രുരുരു

Garden Pirates

In my father's garden there was a sunny corner where he grew berries and vegetables. Every year he cultivated tomatoes, carrots, kale, blueberries, eggplant, lettuce, beets, peas, and beans. All summer long we ate fresh garden produce, straight from the ground. With this bounty, we made delicious meals using recipes from all the places where my husband travelled: Thailand, Italy, Malaysia, Spain, Scotland, and Germany. This sunny little corner brought us great joy, and we daydreamed about it in the winter, when there was nothing to eat but store-bought fruits and vegetables.

One year, thanks to the worm bin and its abundance of compost, we anticipated a particularly successful harvest.

The first to be ready was the kale. We ate it with vinegar and roasted garlic. It was wonderfully tender and sweet. We had high hopes for the peas, and they didn't disappoint. We ate fresh pea soup with bread and cheese. The blueberries would be ripe soon, and we counted the days until blueberry pancakes and blueberry pies. One after another, the berries gradually turned blue. Finally, all was ready and I carried my basket into the garden, excited and hungry.

I couldn't find a single blueberry. Not one.

You can imagine how confused I was. I stared at the bushes. Not only were the ripe berries gone, but the green ones, as well. Only the leaves remained. Who had swiped our harvest? Crows? A raccoon? Coyotes ate berries; maybe the coyotes had eaten our feast. I looked for clues or footprints but couldn't find any. Whoever the thief was, he wasn't easy to trace. Crestfallen, I returned to the house, where we had scrambled eggs for breakfast instead.

Over the next few days, we harvested some carrots and lettuce. As far as our family could tell, no more vegetables were stolen. It seemed a little paranoid to

be preoccupied with the theft of the blueberries, so we didn't talk much about it. Nevertheless, it was on our minds.

The next big harvest would be green beans. We had so many on the vines that we decided to cook a variety of dishes. We discussed Thai beans with hot chilies or maybe Italian bean salad. We invited friends to dinner. Now several families were excited about the ripening beans, suggesting recipes that they shared around. The day of the bean celebration arrived, and my father and I took our baskets into the garden.

Vines are green, and so are beans, so for a moment we thought perhaps the beans were just hiding. But pretty quickly it became clear that we didn't have a single bean. Our harvest had been stolen again. We had a serious problem.

This time, we were determined to catch the thief. Unfortunately, it hadn't been raining so there were no footprints. We thought the puzzle over, looking for clues. The thief hadn't pulled down the vines, therefore it wasn't a raccoon. Raccoons always make a mess of everything. Deer would have also eaten the leaves. Furthermore, despite the dry weather, deer were heavy enough to leave footprints. The thief was not a deer. Would crows or coyotes eat an entire bean harvest? It didn't seem likely. For the first time it occurred to us: maybe the thief was a person.

That night at the feast, all we could talk about was the mystery. While we ate our beans—from the supermarket, and not nearly as good as those from our garden—our friends mulled over the neighbors: who would steal from a garden? Every neighbor was carefully considered: did he or she have motive and means for swiping our berries and vegetables?

Most of the neighbors were friendly and sociable, not the kind of people who would plunder another's garden. But one neighbor was not so dependable. All of our friends knew about the young man who lived kitty-corner from us and who didn't like us. He had a grudge because City Hall had insisted we plant a tree that impeded his view. He held us responsible, even though there had been nothing we could do about it. Furthermore, he was a vegan who worked at the local food co-op; we suspected he could eat a lot of vegetables. Our friends decided he was still mad at us and that he must be the thief. But how could we

catch him red-handed? Nothing else was coming ripe soon in the garden, so we had time to plan. Within a few weeks, it would be the season for tomatoes. By then, we'd have something figured out.

Over the next few weeks, I received a lot of emails from our friends. They threw themselves into figuring out how best to protect our harvest. They suggested everything from walls to video cameras, but my father didn't want his beautiful garden spoiled. Finally, a friend volunteered for night watch. We found him a comfortable lawn chair and hid him in the bushes. We gave him a blanket for his legs. One friend even loaned him night-vision goggles. Our watchman positioned himself and we brought him a large thermos of coffee. No one was going to steal our tomatoes!

Our watchman certainly was alert. After a week, our tomatoes were still hanging on their vines. We were gleeful with victory. We planned a party to make tomato sauce and set a date for the event. The day arrived; another eight hours of sunshine and we'd pick the tomatoes. We went off to work, unconcerned. No one would steal from us in broad daylight. Furthermore, my father would be there. He was a little deaf and prone to catnaps, but he was daunting with a rake in his hand.

When I returned from work my father met me at the door with bad news. He had weeded the garden all morning. Then he'd rested on the patio. He'd only closed his eyes for a moment—he was certain it had been no more than five minutes—and when he awoke, the majority of the harvest had disappeared. There were a few tomatoes left, perhaps enough for one or two small bottles of sauce.

It was unbelievable. Somehow, the thief had gotten away with our vegetables again. I couldn't fathom that anyone, not even the young man kitty-corner from us, would rob us right under our noses. How would he dare? I was so angry, I marched to his house and hammered on the door.

After a few moments, his old mother answered.

"Hello," she said.

"Hi. Is Mr. L. here?" It was hard to control my fury.

"No," she answered. "He's in Texas until next week. Can I help you?"

Uh-oh. Flushed with embarrassment, I murmured my thanks and hurried away. In our rush to accuse someone, we'd apparently made a terrible mistake. Thank heavens my neighbor hadn't been there to bear the brunt of it.

And what came next, after this debacle? We all went to the Spaghetti House for dinner: my father, our friends, my husband, and I. We talked about the thief all night. How did he get off scot-free? We had no idea. When we returned to the house, as expected, the rest of the tomato harvest was gone. We were utterly defeated.

At this point, we gave up. The weeks passed and my father cared for the garden as usual, but we had no illusions that we'd eat the vegetables. It was all very discouraging.

Then one day, just as the eggplants were coming ripe, my father and I were weeding. My neighbor's mother, the one who lived kitty-corner, was walking by and stopped to chat.

"Hello," she said. "What a beautiful garden."

"Thanks," said my father.

"And you have such delightful granddaughters to help you with it."

"Granddaughters?" asked my father, surprised. "I don't have any granddaughters here in Washington."

"But. . . I always see three little girls in your yard. They pick your vegetables, sometimes even late at night. They're hardworking little ones."

"You don't say! And have you noticed where these little girls go with my vegetables?"

"Why, behind your garden shed."

"Thank you. That clears up a lot of things. And how is you son?"

"He's fine. He's back from Texas. I'll tell him you said hello."

And so my father and I went behind the garden shed to see what we could find. There was nothing back there but an old tool chest, which we wrenched open. Inside, we found three wooden swords, three tri-cornered hats—pirate hats—and, underneath, all of our garden produce. They were rotten, naturally: blueberries, beans, and tomatoes, all decaying into a stinking slop. Ugh!

The next day, my father posted a sign in a prominent place in his garden:

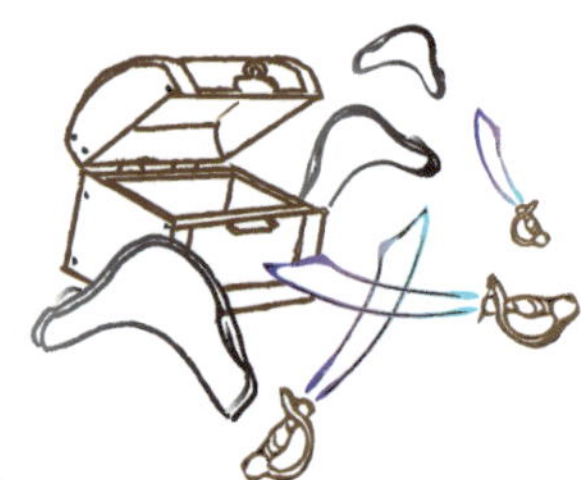

To the Pirates:

With this ransom, I buy back my garden. From now on, please use your swords to protect my vegetables instead of plundering them.

Thank you,

O.T. Murphy

He attached three gift cards to the sign, made out for the local ice cream parlor.

The swords and hats disappeared from the tool box that next night. We never did catch the pirates in the act. Perhaps they now protect the garden, or maybe they just leave it alone. In any case, we didn't have our berries or vegetables stolen again.

"Next year," said my father, "I'll put out ransom in the spring and save us a world of trouble."

So that's what we do every year, and we grow our vegetables in peace.

ʘʘʘ

About the Author

Lisa Murphy is a family physician who writes in a variety of genres, including magical realism, sci-fi, short fiction, and historical fiction. She is the author of *The Wyrmstone* and *The Turkish Mirror.* She lives near Seattle, Washington with her family. In her free time, she tends an unruly and glorious garden with her father.

About the Illustrator

Liza Brown is a designer and soprano who loves helping people find their voice through art and music. She loves living in Seattle near family and water. When not designing or singing, she studies the neurological impact of addiction on the brain and develops treatment methods through art and music.

www.ingramcontent.com/pod-product-compliance
Lightning Source LLC
Chambersburg PA
CBHW041418300726
48981CB00007B/332